Is this ghost for real?

The girls were too scared to scream. They were too frozen with fear to run.

"Woof!" Chip barked. She jumped out of Dr. Funk-n-Stine's arms and ran straight to Nancy.

"G-g-good girl!" Nancy stammered.

She scooped Chip up and ran with her friends out of the TV station. Mrs. Marvin's car was waiting for them.

"That was him," George said as they raced to the car. "That was Dr. Funk-n-Stine!"

"He said he would be back," added Bess.

Nancy hugged her puppy tight. She didn't want to believe in ghosts. But seeing was believing. And she was pretty sure she had just seen the ghost of Dr. Funk-n-Stine!

Join the CLUE CREW
& solve these other cases!

Nancy Drew

#9 AND The CLUE CREW™

The Halloween Hoax

BY CAROLYN KEENE

ILLUSTRATED BY MACKY PAMINTUAN

Aladdin Paperbacks
New York London Toronto Sydney

This book is a work of fiction. Any references to historical events, real people, or real locales are used fictitiously. Other names, characters, places, and incidents are the product of the author's imagination, and any resemblance to actual events or locales or persons, living or dead, is entirely coincidental.

6♟ ALADDIN PAPERBACKS

An imprint of Simon & Schuster Children's Publishing Division

1230 Avenue of the Americas, New York, NY 10020

Text copyright © 2007 by Simon & Schuster, Inc.

Illustrations copyright © 2007 by Macky Pamintuan

All rights reserved, including the right of reproduction in whole or in part in any form.

ALADDIN PAPERBACKS, NANCY DREW, and colophon are registered trademarks of Simon & Schuster, Inc.

NANCY DREW AND THE CLUE CREW is a trademark of Simon & Schuster, Inc.

Designed by Lisa Vega.

The text of this book was set in ITC Stone Informal.

Manufactured in the United States of America

First Aladdin Paperbacks edition August 2007

10 9 8

Library of Congress Control Number 2007921782

ISBN-13: 978-1-4169-3664-0

ISBN-10: 1-4169-3664-5

0211 OFF

CONTENTS

CHAPTER ONE

TV Trouble

"Hey, Nancy," George Fayne said, cracking a smile. "Your tail is 'dragon.'"

Eight-year-old Nancy Drew glanced back. The tail of her dragon costume was hanging over the bench and *dragging* on the floor.

"Dragging. Dragon. I get it." Nancy giggled.

Bess Marvin reached down to tie her ballet slipper. She was dressed as a ballerina in a pink tutu.

"What could be better than wearing our Halloween costumes four whole days before Halloween?" Bess asked.

The tin cans on George's homemade robot costume clanked together as she moved.

"Wearing our Halloween costumes *and* being on the *Dudley the Science Dude* show!" she said.

Nancy high-fived her two best friends. The girls were sitting in a real live TV studio with the rest of their third-grade class. Their teacher, Mrs. Ramirez, had gotten them surprise tickets for Dudley's special Halloween show. Dudley was a cool scientist who performed awesome experiments on TV.

Nancy looked past the TV cameras and lights at Dudley's laboratory. The set looked just like it did on TV. The counter was filled with test tubes and microscopes. Jars were stuffed with animal teeth, shells, and rocks. There were maps on the walls and computers with science information flashing on their screens.

"Where is Dudley, anyway?" Andrea Wu complained. Andrea was dressed as Little Bo Peep. Her best friend, Kayla Bruce, was dressed as her sheep.

Quincy Taylor's caterpillar costume crunched as he wiggled on the bench. "By the time the show starts I'll be a butterfly!" he groaned.

"Dudley will be here," Shelby Metcalf declared as she stood up. She was dressed up like Dudley, in a yellow lab coat and blue goggles. "In the meantime—who wants to join my Dudley the Science Dude Fan Club? We'll meet at my house every week and do one of Dudley's experiments."

"The gross ones?" Peter Patino asked.

"For sure!" replied Shelby.

Some hands shot up. Shelby looked at Nancy, Bess, and George. "Don't you want to join my club too?" she asked.

"Thanks, but we already have a club," Nancy admitted.

"It's called the Clue Crew," added George.

"We solve mysteries," Bess explained.

"Oh, that!" Shelby smiled as she remembered. "But solving mysteries can't be as fun as growing a fungus on dirty gym socks!"

"Eww," Bess said, making a face.

Deirdre Shannon's pointed princess hat

shifted as she tossed her hair behind her shoulders. "How do we know Dudley is a *real* scientist?" she asked. "He's probably just an actor who plays one on TV."

Shelby's eyes flashed. "Sure he's a real scientist," she insisted. "Last week he turned a penny green. An actor can't do that."

A woman holding a clipboard walked over. "Hello, kids," she said. "My name is Valerie, and I'm a producer. That means I help Dudley plan all his shows."

The class sat at attention as Valerie spoke.

"There are four studios inside Station WRIV-TV," Valerie explained. "You're in the studio that tapes *Dudley the Science Dude* every week."

Next Valerie introduced the crew. Mike, Fran, and Bill were stagehands. They set up Dudley's experiments and props. Sam was the director. He chose which scenes the people at home watched on TV. He also made sure the show went as planned. The stage manager's name was Lisa. "Lisa's job is to tell Dudley when to start talking and when to stop," Valerie explained.

"Maybe Lisa can tell Peter to stop talking in class," Marcy Rubin snickered.

"Very funny," Peter muttered.

"Now here's someone you all know," Valerie announced.

Excited whispers filled the studio as Kirby Kessler ran over to Valerie. Kirby was Dudley's ten-year-old helper on the show. He usually wore jeans and a T-shirt. But today he wore a long black cape for Halloween.

"These kids must be in third grade," Kirby said.

"How did you know?" Valerie asked.

Kirby turned to show a hump under his cape. "I had a hunch!" he joked.

A few kids laughed. A few groaned. "Good one," George said with a chuckle.

"It's him!" Shelby shouted. "It's Dudley!"

The kids cheered as Dudley suddenly ran across the studio toward the audience. His lab coat was decorated with a spider design for Halloween.

"Did you know a handshake is science too?" Dudley asked as he shook Shelby's hand. "I just passed hundreds of germs from my hand to yours."

"Oh, thank you," Shelby gushed. "I am never going to wash this hand again. Ever!"

Next, to get the audience excited and because Halloween was on the way, Dudley held a screaming contest. Everyone got a chance to give his or her best scream. Bess's scream sounded more like a squeak. Kevin Garcia gave a good scream until his fake vampire fangs fell out. But when Nadine "the Drama Queen" Nardo screamed, everyone covered their ears.

"We have a winner!" said Dudley. He

snapped his fingers. Kirby ran to Nadine, handing her a Dudley button as a prize.

"Mr. Dudley? Mr. Dudley?" George called. "Can you sign my sneaker, please?"

"Sure," Dudley said. He snapped his fingers again. Kirby handed a pen to Dudley. He quickly scribbled his name on George's sneaker.

"Wow!" George exclaimed as Dudley walked over to the cameras. "I'm never going to wash this sneaker either."

"Since when do you *ever* wash your sneakers, George?" Bess said with a sigh.

George stuck her tongue out at Bess. Sometimes Nancy couldn't believe they were cousins.

"Ready to tape," Lisa shouted.

"This is it," Nancy whispered excitedly.

The lights on the ceiling flashed brighter. Lisa turned to Dudley and began to count down: "Five . . . four . . . three . . . two . . ."

"It's Dudley the Science Dude's Halloween show!" an announcer's voice boomed. "Kids, give it up for Dudley!"

Everyone cheered as Dudley ran onto the set.

"Happy Halloween, you guys," he declared. "In our audience today we have kids from River Heights Elementary School, and they are ready for some creepy and fun-tastic experiments!"

"Yeah!" Nancy's class shouted.

"And wait till we check out those pains in the neck, our friends the bats!" Dudley went on.

Excited whispers filled the studio.

"But what would Halloween be without a bubbly witch's brew?" asked Dudley. He held two bottles over a bowl. "The secret recipe is baking soda, vinegar—and a dash of spooky glow-in-the-dark green paint!"

Everyone watched as Dudley poured the green-colored vinegar and baking soda into the bowl. The mixture began to fizz and foam until—

"Whoa!" Dudley cried as he jumped back. The fizzy brew was oozing out of the bowl and across the counter!

"Neat!" Kevin laughed.

But Nancy noticed that Dudley wasn't laughing. When the cameras stopped rolling, he stared at the icky green puddle on the floor.

"That wasn't supposed to happen," Dudley said. "I measured the right amount of ingredients before the show."

"Some scientist," Deirdre muttered.

Shelby heard Deirdre and jumped to her feet. "Yay, Dudley!" she cheered. "That experiment was truly awesome!"

"Let's move on to the next one," Valerie suggested.

"Three . . . two . . . one," Lisa said. She pointed to Dudley, and he smiled into the camera.

"Did you ever try to squeeze an egg into a bottle?" Dudley asked. "I know it sounds weird, but it can be done!"

Dudley picked up an egg and—*crack*—it smashed in his hand. "Huh? What's going on?" he said. He sounded puzzled.

A door flew open. Sam the director marched into the studio. "That egg was supposed to be hard-boiled," he said.

"It was," Bill, one of the stagehands, said. "I boiled it myself this morning."

Nancy didn't get it. Dudley's experiments never went wrong.

Her thoughts were interrupted by one of Nadine's prize-winning screams. Nadine's hand shook as she pointed up to the ceiling.

"B-b-b-b-," she stammered.

Nancy and her classmates looked up.

They screamed too. Fluttering near the ceiling were at least a dozen real live *bats*!

CHAPTER TWO

Spirit on the Set!

"Bats get stuck in your hair!" Madison Foley cried.

"Bats suck blood," Kevin said. "Cool!"

Dudley tried to keep everybody calm. "Bats are very helpful creatures!" he babbled. "Did you know they can eat up to six hundred mosquitoes in an hour?"

"How many kids can they eat?" Quincy asked.

The stagehands chased the bats with nets.

"I know I put the lid on the bat house," said Fran, swinging a net. "What happened to it?"

Mrs. Ramirez ran into the studio. She had been sitting in a waiting room, watching the show on a monitor.

"I'm sorry, Mrs. Ramirez," Valerie said. "We'll have to stop taping for the day. There are too many problems."

"Can we come back another time?" Shelby asked.

Mrs. Ramirez shook her head and said, "I don't think so. This TV show doesn't seem safe for children."

"Awwww!" the kids groaned.

"Sorry, kids," Dudley called. He gave a nervous chuckle. "I guess the studio must be haunted or something."

Mrs. Ramirez led the class out of the studio and into the hall.

"Look," Bess said. She pointed down at Nancy's dragon tail. "You dragged your tail through Dudley's brew puddle on the way out."

"Yuck!" Nancy said, lifting her drippy tail.

"You're so lucky, Nancy," Shelby said, her eyes shining. "Now you'll have a souvenir from Dudley's show."

"I told you Dudley wasn't a real scientist," Deirdre scoffed. "He can't even boil an egg."

"Dudley is a dud!" Peter laughed.

"I don't want to join his fan club anymore," Kayla said to Shelby.

"But it wasn't Dudley's fault," Shelby insisted. "You heard what he said—the studio is haunted."

"Prove it," Peter challenged.

Shelby's eyes darted around as she thought. Suddenly she pointed at Nancy, Bess, and George. "I can't prove it," she said. "But I know the Clue Crew can!"

"What?" Nancy cried.

"Class," Mrs. Ramirez called. "Keep walking double-file with your partners."

Shelby ran next to Nancy. Bess and George walked right behind them.

"We can't prove Dudley's studio is haunted, Shelby," Nancy whispered. "We don't even believe in ghosts."

"You don't *have* to believe in them," Shelby said. "You just have to find the ghosts who messed things up."

"We're detectives," George said. "Not ghost hunters."

Shelby's big brown eyes filled with tears. "Thanks a lot," she muttered. "Now nobody will join my fan club."

Nancy's heart sank. The Clue Crew liked to help others by solving mysteries. And Shelby needed their help. So . . .

"No problem, Shelby," Nancy said. "We'll do it."

Shelby brushed a tear from her cheek and smiled. "Thanks, you guys!" she said. "But don't do it for me—do it for Dudley the Science Dude!"

Shelby skipped ahead slightly.

"Why did you say yes, Nancy?" George asked.

"Don't worry," Nancy said. "Shelby will forget about everything once we don't find any ghosts."

"What if we *do* find ghosts?" Bess asked.

Nancy stared at Bess. "Don't tell me you believe in ghosts too," she said.

"Anything is possible," Bess said with a shrug. "Especially around Halloween."

Nancy wasn't worried. She knew they wouldn't find ghosts in Dudley's studio. After all, they were the Clue Crew—not the Boo Crew!

It was a cool sunny Saturday as Nancy sat in the kitchen eating a bowl of Squirrel Nuts cereal. Hannah Gruen stood at the kitchen sink, scrubbing Nancy's dragon costume.

Hannah was the Drew's housekeeper. She'd been helping out Mr. Drew since Nancy was three years old. That's how old Nancy was when her mother died.

"I couldn't get the green stain out," Hannah said. "But at least it matches the rest of your dragon costume."

"Thanks, Hannah," said Nancy.

Mr. Drew walked into the kitchen. He was wearing corduroy pants and his favorite Saturday sweatshirt, not the usual suit he wore to his lawyer job during the week.

"Can you breathe fire yet, Miss Dragon?" Mr. Drew asked with a wink.

"Still working on it, Daddy," Nancy said.

"Maybe I should cook my famous spicy barbecue meatballs," Hannah joked. "That should do the trick."

A car horn honked outside. It was Mrs. Fayne in her catering van. She had agreed to drive the girls to the WRIV-TV station so they could look for clues.

Nancy gave her dad and Hannah a good-bye kiss. She had told them all about her new case the night before.

"Why don't you just ask the others at the TV station if they think it's haunted?" Mr. Drew asked. "Wouldn't that be easier?"

"Sure," Nancy said. She took one last sip of

her milk. "But it wouldn't be as much fun!"

Nancy ran outside and climbed into Mrs. Fayne's van. As she squeezed between a stack of platters and her friends, she noticed that the van smelled like pickles.

"Good morning!" Bess said cheerily.

Nancy's eyes widened when she saw Bess. Her friend was wearing a weird-looking pair of goggles. The lenses made Bess's eyes look twice their size!

"What are *those*?" Nancy asked.

"They're ghost goggles I built myself," Bess said. "Now I'll be able to see ghosts in the dark."

Nancy smiled. Bess loved to fix and build things more than anything.

"I brought a compass," George told Nancy. She held up a round device that looked like a watch. "I looked up ghost hunting on the computer." Nancy nodded. George knew more about finding information on the computer than anyone else Nancy knew. "The needle will spin out of control if there's a ghost in the room . . . not that I believe in ghosts," George added.

"I brought stuff too," Nancy said. She opened her small backpack. "My plastic clue bag as usual. And this. . . ."

Nancy pulled out a writing pad. The first page had a line drawn down the middle to form two columns. Over the first column Nancy wrote *Ghosts*. Over the second, *No Ghosts*.

"Every time we find a clue we will put it into one of these two columns. The column with the most clues will win," Nancy explained. "And I have a feeling which one that will be."

Mrs. Fayne dropped the girls off in front of the WRIV-TV building. While she delivered platters to a store down the street, the girls filed into the station.

"Remember," George whispered, "we're here to see Dudley. He's the one who thinks his studio is haunted."

Bess pulled off her ghost goggles as they walked across the lobby. A guard sitting behind a desk looked up and smiled. Nancy read the nameplate on the desk: BEATRICE ARMSTRONG

"May we see Dudley, please?" Nancy said.

"Dudley doesn't work here on weekends," Beatrice replied.

The girls stepped away from the desk.

"We have to get into Dudley's studio," Nancy whispered. "But how will we do that without Dudley?"

A young man stepped into the lobby. He looked around and said, "Okay! Who's here for a tour of the TV station?"

A few people stepped forward.

"We are!" George blurted.

"We are?" Bess asked.

George raised an eyebrow at Bess. Soon the girls were following the tour all the way down the hall.

"My name is Brad," said the man. "Our first stop will be the newsroom, where you'll all meet Sy the Weather Guy!"

Nancy recognized a door with creepy crawlies

painted all over it. "This is the place," she said in a whisper.

The girls slipped away from the tour and inside Dudley's studio. The set looked just like it had the day before. Except the bat house was gone, and the test tubes on the counter were filled with colorful liquids.

Bess put on her ghost goggles and looked around. She pointed to the floor. "Ghost footprints!" she exclaimed.

Nancy looked down. She didn't need Bess's goggles to see two green footprints on the floor—and they seemed to be glowing!

George held up her compass. The needle was spinning around wildly. "There *are* ghosts in this studio!" she said.

Nancy groaned under her breath. Now George was starting to believe in ghosts too!

"There's got to be a reason for everything," Nancy told her friends.

"While you look for reasons," said Bess, "I'll look for more ghost footprints in the back."

She walked to the back of the studio. Nancy and George inspected the counter. Next to the test tubes they found a small piece of paper.

George picked up the paper and studied it.

"These words are pretty long," she said. "It must be the formula for some science experiment."

"Maybe Dudley wrote it," Nancy guessed.

George held the formula next to her autographed sneaker. "The handwriting on the note doesn't match Dudley's signature," she said. "So it can't be his."

Nancy pointed to a blue fingerprint on the paper. "Whose fingerprint is that?" she asked. "What do you think, Bess?"

No answer.

"Bess?" Nancy called. She turned and looked around. Bess was nowhere in sight!

CHAPTER THREE

A Secret Room

Nancy and George darted around the studio looking for Bess. They searched under tables, around cameras, even behind a life-size cardboard cutout of Dudley.

"Maybe the ghosts got her," George said.

"Stop it, George!" Nancy hissed. She felt her heart pound as she leaned against the back wall. "She couldn't have just disappeared like—"

She gasped as the wall behind her began to swing back. She grabbed George's arm, and the two spun around with the wall.

"Whoooooaaaaaaaa!" Nancy and George cried.

The wall stopped spinning. Nancy and George stumbled forward into a small room. It was jam-packed with cardboard boxes and racks of clothes.

"How did we end up here?" asked George.

Nancy was dizzy but not worried. "A trick wall! The wall was probably part of Dudley's set," she said. "Strange things happen on TV all the time."

"Then what happened to Bess?" George wondered.

"I don't know," Nancy said, looking around nervously. Suddenly they heard a noise.

CLUNK . . . CLUNK . . . CLUNK . . .

Nancy and George froze as the sound got louder and louder. It sounded like heavy footsteps. Suddenly Bess popped out from behind a clothing rack.

"Bess!" Nancy said, smiling with relief.

"How do you like this secret room?" said Bess. "And check out this groovy stuff!" She wore a floppy hat on her head and clunky platform shoes on her feet.

"Groovy?" Nancy asked.

"It means cool," Bess said. "My mom uses that word sometimes."

Nancy scanned the room, reached into a box near her foot, and pulled out a poster. On it was a yellow smiley face and the words "Have a Nice Day!"

Next she flipped through a rack of clothes. She found bell-bottom pants, colorful mini-dresses, and faded jeans with patches sewn all over. One satin jacket had RIVER HEIGHTS HIGH, CLASS OF '78 across the back.

"This stuff is from the 1970s," said Nancy.

"That's ancient history!" Bess cried.

George held up two black discs, each with a hole in the middle. "These are called records," she explained. "My mom and dad still have a few."

"Do your parents have these, too?" Bess gulped. She had picked up two jars. One was filled with pairs of fangs. The other was packed to the rim with rubber eyeballs.

"Creepy!" Nancy said. As she hung up the satin jacket, something else fell off the rack. It was an orange-colored lab coat. Written across the back was "Dr. Funk-n-Stine."

"Who is Dr. Funk-n-Stine?" Nancy asked. Suddenly the girls heard a loud noise.

BOOM! FIZZZZZ!

They all jumped.

"What was that?" George whispered.

"It's coming from behind the wall," Nancy murmured.

The girls ran to the trick wall. They pushed on it, and the wall spun around. Soon they stumbled back into Dudley's studio.

Nancy gasped when she saw the test tubes on the counter. The colorful liquids they'd seen before were now bubbling and fizzing over the rims. "They weren't doing that when we came in," she said.

"Maybe the ghost did it," Bess suggested. "The same ghost who left the green footprints."

The girls jumped as the studio door swung open. Brad the tour guide was leading his group into the studio.

"This is where we tape *Dudley the Science Dude*," Brad said. He stopped when he saw the out-of-control test tubes. "Cheese and crackers—what's up with that?"

Bess kicked off the platform shoes. "We were just leaving," she said. She shoved the floppy hat into Brad's hands. Then Nancy, Bess, and George raced out of the studio.

"What happened?" Mrs. Fayne asked as the girls jumped into the van. "You girls look like you saw a ghost!"

"Just his footprints, Mom," George told her.

Bess turned to Nancy. "Write all the stuff we saw today in your Ghosts column, Nancy," she said.

"Don't forget about this," said George. She held up a piece of paper. "I grabbed that science formula on the way out."

"Are you sure it's the formula?" Nancy asked.

"Sure I'm sure," George answered. But when she glanced down at the paper, her eyes popped wide open.

"What's the matter, George?" asked Nancy.

"The blue fingerprint is still there," George replied. "But the whole science formula has *disappeared*!"

CHAPTER FOUR

Funk-n-Stine Online

"How could a whole science formula vanish?" Nancy wondered as she paced across the purple rug in her bedroom. "Think hard."

"I'm thinking so hard my brain hurts," Bess said.

It was Sunday morning. The Clue Crew was working on the case in Nancy's bedroom. Her room was also their Clue Crew headquarters, with a special drawer in Nancy's desk for their clues and a computer for research.

"They sell trick pens with disappearing ink," George said. "I saw some in a joke shop once."

"But what about all the other stuff we found

in the back room?" asked Nancy. "And who was Dr. Funk-n-Stine?"

"Let's find out," George said, turning to the computer. She went online and searched for Dr. Funk-n-Stine. A colorful website soon appeared on the screen.

"What does it say?" Bess asked.

"'This site is dedicated to Dr. Funk-n-Stine,'" George read aloud. "'And his groovy show.'"

George clicked on a picture of a TV set. A photo of a bunch of kids appeared. They were dancing in bell-bottom pants and platform shoes.

"Those are the clothes we saw in the secret room!" Nancy pointed out.

"It looks like they're in some haunted lab," said George. "Check out the cobwebs and jars filled with creepy stuff. Just like the jars we found yesterday."

A man in the picture wore an orange lab coat and clunky-looking boots. His hair stuck out wildly like a dandelion puff.

"That must be Dr. Funk-n-Stine," Nancy said.

"He must have been a scientist like Dudley."

"You mean a *mad* scientist," George joked.

The girls giggled as a tune began to play: "Get up, get grooooovy! With Dr. Funk-n-Stine!"

Nancy, Bess, and George read as much as they could about Dr. Funk-n-Stine. He used to have his own science show on TV. The name of the show was *Dr. Funk-n-Stine's Groovy Mad Lab*. It always had lots of commercials for

Baxter's Licorice Gum. The show ran from 1975 to 1979.

"It says Dr. Funk-n-Stine was very sad when his show ended," George said. "As he left the TV station, he promised he'd be back someday."

"What happened to him?" said Bess.

George leaned forward to read on. "It says he went to the Great Beyond," she told the others.

"What's the Great Beyond?" Nancy asked.

"I think it's a nice way of saying he died," George explained.

The girls were silent. Until Bess shouted, "That's it! That's it! Dudley's studio is being haunted by the ghost of Dr. Funk-n-Stine!"

"What?" cried Nancy.

Bess ran to her pink backpack on Nancy's bed. She pulled out a gadget that looked like two cups attached to a headband. "We have to go back to the studio so I can try out my new Spirit Sounds," she declared. "Maybe I'll hear the ghost of Dr. Funk-n-Stine."

Nancy didn't think the studio was haunted

by Dr. Funk-n-Stine—or any ghost. But she did want to find the real reason for Dudley's goofed experiments once and for all!

"Okay," she said. "But how will we get into the studio this time?"

George pointed to Nancy's dragon costume hanging behind her door. "We can pretend we're trick-or-treating!"

"Halloween isn't until Tuesday," Nancy pointed out.

"We'll say we want to get a head start!" said George.

"What do you think, Nancy?" Bess asked.

Nancy smiled. She couldn't wait to wear her dragon costume again—even with the yucky green stain!

"I still don't think we'll find any ghosts," Nancy admitted. "But a head start on Halloween is pretty cool!"

Bess and George ran home to put on their costumes. When they returned to Nancy's house, Mr. Drew drove the girls to the TV station.

"Remember," Mr. Drew told them. "No eating tons of candy before Halloween."

"We're not going for candy, Daddy," said Nancy. "We're going for clues."

Mr. Drew parked in front of WRIV-TV. As the girls climbed out of the car, he said, "I'll be in the hardware store down the block. Wait for me in front of the station in twenty minutes."

Each girl held her own trick-or-treat bag. Bess secretly carried her Spirit Sounds inside hers. They filed into the TV station and shouted, "Trick or treat!"

A different guard sat behind the desk that day. Her nameplate read ROSALIE VITALE.

"You're a bit early, girls," Rosalie said.

"We want to get a head start," Bess blurted out. "Before the best treats are gone!"

"Good idea." Rosalie chuckled. "I see we have a dragon, a ballerina, and the Tin Man from *The Wizard of Oz*."

"I'm actually a robot," said George.

Rosalie pointed to a glass jar on her desk.

"Help yourselves to some candy, kids," she said. "Don't be shy."

The girls stared at the candy jar. They needed to get *inside* the TV station.

"Um," Nancy said slowly, "do you have a . . . candy machine in the back?"

"We only eat granola bars," Bess added. "Maybe there's some in your candy machine—"

"In the back," George put in.

"Picky, picky, picky." Rosalie sighed.

A boy with blond hair ran past the desk and down the hall. It was Kirby Kessler!

"Kirby, wait up!" Nancy called.

Kirby stopped and turned around. "What?" he asked.

"Um—can you sign my sneaker?" George asked quickly.

"You want *my* autograph?" gasped Kirby. He whipped out a pen and smiled. "Sure—come on over!"

"Go ahead." Rosalie waved them through.

The girls ran straight to Kirby. George stuck

out her foot and said, "You can make it out to George, please."

"Isn't George a boy's name?" Kirby asked.

"It's really Georgia," Bess said, smiling. "But she hates being called by her full name."

George nudged Bess with her elbow.

"When I have my own TV show, I'm going to sign a ton of autographs," Kirby told the girls as he signed George's sneaker.

Nancy nodded. Kirby *was* funny enough to have his own show someday. But then she noticed something else about Kirby: His face was covered with gray smudges.

"What happened to your face, Kirby?" Nancy asked.

Kirby's hand flew up to his cheek. "Uh . . . I'm going trick-or-treating too," he said. "As a chimney sweep!"

Kirby dropped the pen into his pocket. Then he ran down the hall and around the corner.

"At least we got into the station," George said.

Nancy, Bess, and George hurried toward

Dudley's studio. People in the hall stopped to smile at their costumes. One woman dropped wrapped candies into their bags.

When no one was watching, the girls slipped into Dudley's studio. There was nobody inside. But something wasn't right. . . .

"Are we in the right place?" asked George.

Nancy looked around. They were in a science lab. But this one was covered with cobwebs. Its shelves were stocked with glass jars filled with eyeballs, snakes, and vampire fangs. There was even a skull with glowing red eyes!

"This doesn't look like Dudley's set," exclaimed Bess.

"No," Nancy said with a gulp. "It looks like Dr. Funk-n-Stine's Groovy Mad Lab!"

ChaPTER FiVE

Fright in the Night

Nancy jumped as a fake spider dropped onto her shoulder. She still didn't believe in ghosts . . . not really.

George's tin cans clanked as she walked around the studio. "What's that?" she asked, pointing to a tall, oval-shaped case. A face on the lid was painted in gold.

"I think it's a sar-co-pha-gus," Nancy said, pronouncing the word carefully. "They built them in ancient Egypt to hold mummies."

"How do you know?" asked Bess.

"I saw one in a museum once," Nancy replied.

"I smell licorice," George said, wrinkling her nose.

"Baxter's Licorice Gum!" Bess gasped. "Those were the commercials on Dr. Funk-n-Stine's old TV show!"

"Smells are a sign of ghosts," George said. "I read that on the computer too."

Bess pulled her Spirit Sounds from her trick-or-treat bag and slipped them over her ears. "I think I hear music," she said.

Nancy and George heard it too.

"Get up . . . get grooovy! With Dr. Funk-n-Stine!"

"It's the Dr. Funk-n-Stine show tune!" Bess cried. "Let's get out of here!"

Bess stuffed her Spirit Sounds back into her trick-or-treat bag. Then the girls charged toward the door. Nancy stopped running when she heard footsteps out in the hall.

"Someone's coming!" she hissed. "Hide!"

The girls scurried around the studio looking for a place to hide. George raced to the sarcophagus and yanked open the lid. She shrieked as a mummy wrapped in bandages tumbled on top of her.

"I want my mummy—I mean mommy!" George screamed as she pushed the mummy off.

The girls burst out of the studio. They ran past Valerie, Dudley's producer, standing outside the door.

"What were you doing in there?" Valerie demanded.

"Trick or treat!" Bess shouted as they kept running.

The girls clutched their trick-or-treat bags as they raced outside.

"Not only did Dr. Funk-n-Stine come back," George said, catching her breath, "he brought his whole show, too!"

"Now do you believe in ghosts, Nancy?" Bess asked.

Nancy didn't answer. As they waited for Mr. Drew to pick them up, she filled in her Ghosts column with the latest clues. Her No Ghosts column was totally blank.

Maybe Bess and George are right, Nancy thought. *Maybe there are such things as ghosts.*

For the rest of the day Nancy couldn't think about anything else. As her dad tucked her into bed, she asked, "Daddy, do you believe in ghosts?"

"Only on Halloween," Mr. Drew answered. "Why?"

Nancy sat straight up. She explained all the

weird things the Clue Crew had found in Dudley's studio—the music, the footprint, the licorice smell, and the spinning compass.

"Was there a lot of electrical equipment in the studio?" Mr. Drew asked. "Cables and wires on the floor?"

"Yes," Nancy said.

"That might explain the compass," Mr. Drew said. "Compasses pick up energy from surrounding power sources."

"You think?" Nancy asked excitedly. She felt a little relieved.

"Pretty sure," Mr. Drew said. He leaned over and kissed Nancy good night. Before he closed the door, Nancy's Labrador puppy, Chocolate Chip, slipped into the room.

"You don't have to guard my bed, Chip." Nancy giggled. "I'm not that scared anymore."

Nancy felt better as she switched off her lamp. If electricity made the compass needle spin, there had to an explanation for all those other things too.

She was about to snuggle under her quilt when she spotted something across her room—something green and glowing in the dark!

ChaPTER Six

Chip on the Case

Nancy gasped. What could be green and glowing in her bedroom?

Her hand trembled as she reached for her lamp. When she switched on the light, the green glow was gone. In its place was her dragon costume, still hanging behind the door.

Chip padded after Nancy as she walked over to her dragon costume. As she picked up the tail, something clicked in her mind.

"The *green stain* was glowing, Chip," Nancy said with relief. "The one I got from Dudley's witch's brew puddle."

Nancy remembered that Dudley used glow-in-the-dark paint in his experiment. Suddenly

she remembered something else—the glowing green footprints in Dudley's studio.

"Maybe Dudley stepped in the puddle by mistake," Nancy thought out loud. "Maybe those were *his* footprints."

Nancy was on a roll. She pulled out her writing pad. Then she began writing more possible reasons next to each Ghosts clue.

"Dr. Funk-n-Stine's Groovy Mad Lab," Nancy read from her list. She snapped her fingers. "Maybe the people at the station decorated the studio for a Halloween party."

One by one Nancy thought of reasons for each Ghosts clue. But as she got to the last one, she closed her eyes and fell asleep.

"Well?" Shelby asked. "How many ghosts did you find?"

It was Monday morning. The girls were standing in the school yard waiting for the bell to ring.

"You're not going to like this, Shelby," Nancy said. "But we didn't—"

"There's one more thing we have to check out!" George cut in.

Nancy stared at George. *What thing?* she wondered.

"What do you mean?" Shelby asked.

"Trust us, Shelby," said George.

Shelby shrugged and walked away.

"George!" Nancy said. "I wanted to tell Shelby that the studio was *not* haunted!"

"After all those weird things we saw and heard?" Bess cried.

"No problem," Nancy said with a grin. "Last night I figured out reasons for everything that happened."

Bess and George listened as Nancy explained the reasons for the green glowing footprints, the spinning needle on George's compass, and the Halloween decorations.

"What about that licorice smell?" Bess asked.

"Easy," Nancy said. "All those fake black spiders were probably made out of licorice."

"What about the music we heard?" asked George.

"Remember that skull with the glowing eyes?" Nancy said. "It was probably a music box."

Bess and George exchanged looks that said they didn't buy it.

"Okay, how do you explain the bubbling test tubes?" Bess asked.

"Can't," Nancy admitted. "That's when I fell asleep."

"Whatever," George said. "I still want to go back to the TV station. And I want you to bring Chocolate Chip."

Nancy couldn't believe her ears. "I hope you mean cookies or ice cream," she said. "Because I'm not bringing my puppy to the TV station."

"Please, Nancy," George pleaded. "I saw a movie on TV last night. This little dog was the only one in the house who could see ghosts. He barked like crazy whenever a ghost was in the room!"

"I think we should try it," Bess said.

Nancy pressed her lips together to keep from saying no. She didn't want to do it. But the Clue Crew was a team. And that meant teamwork.

"Okay, okay." Nancy sighed. "But the only thing that makes Chip bark like crazy is squirrels."

It was hard for Nancy not to think about the case during school. In the class spelling bee she spelled the word "ghost" instead of "boast." She found herself humming Dr. Funk-n-Stine's tune on the lunch line. She even had an uncanny craving for licorice.

Just one more trip to the studio, Nancy thought. *And this case will be closed. Once and for all!*

After school Mrs. Marvin drove the girls and Chip to the TV station.

"Are you sure you don't want me to come inside with you?" Mrs. Marvin called from her car window. "What if the station doesn't allow dogs?"

"They will, Mom," Bess said. "Who doesn't like cute little puppies?"

Nancy held Chip's leash tightly as they filed into the TV station. A guard named Earl was sitting behind the desk this time. He took one look at Chip and said, "No dogs allowed in the station."

"Not even cute ones?" Bess asked.

A woman with curly black hair rushed over to the desk. She was wearing a white smock and holding a spray can.

"Coco, at last!" the woman gasped. "I thought she'd never get here."

"Coco?" Nancy said.

"I'm Lucinda. I'll be getting Coco ready for her segment," Lucinda said. "Follow me!"

Lucinda scooped Chip into her arms. Her high-heeled shoes made tap-tap-tapping noises as they walked briskly down the hall.

"Who's Coco?" Nancy whispered.

"Who cares?" George whispered back. "We're in!"

They were halfway down the hall when Nancy spotted Kirby. The strands of his blond hair were sticking way up in the air.

"Hi, Kirby," Nancy said. "New haircut?"

"Gotta go!" Kirby blurted. He turned and slipped into one of the studios.

"Bess? George?" Nancy asked. "Did you see Kirby? He looked like a porcupine!"

"Forget Kirby," said George. "Look at Chip!"

George pointed inside the makeup room. Chip was sitting in one of the chairs while

Lucinda sprayed her with pink glitter.

"What are you doing to my dog?" Nancy demanded.

"Coco is going to be on the five o'clock news," Lucinda explained. "They're doing a segment on Halloween makeup that's safe for dogs."

Another woman appeared at the door. In her arms was a little white dog with a ruby collar.

"What is *that* dog doing here?" she exclaimed, pointing to Chip. "Coco and I drove two hours just to be here today!"

Lucinda froze with the can in her hand. "Coco?" she exclaimed. She looked at Chocolate Chip. "Then who's this?"

"Coco's understudy," George said quickly.

Chip barked and jumped off the chair. She shot right past Nancy and out the door.

"Chip—come back!" Nancy cried.

People stopped to stare as Nancy, Bess, and George chased Chip down the hall.

"She's going crazy!" George said as they ran. "Just like that dog in the movie."

"Maybe she saw a ghost!" Bess panted.

"No way!" said Nancy. "That woman must have scared her, that's all."

Chip slid on the floor as she rounded the corner. The three girls ran around the corner too. They skidded to a stop when they saw a man with wild hair and a bright orange lab coat. The man laughed as he held Chocolate Chip.

"Mwah, hah, hah," he said. "Cute puppy!"

Nancy gulped as she recognized the man at once.

"Dr. Funk-n-Stine!"

CHAPTER SEVEN

Follow That Ghost!

The girls were too scared to scream. They were too frozen with fear to run.

"Woof!" Chip barked. She jumped out of Dr. Funk-n-Stine's arms and ran straight to Nancy.

"G-g-good girl!" Nancy stammered.

She scooped Chip up and ran with her friends out of the TV station. Mrs. Marvin's car was waiting for them.

"That was him," George said as they raced to the car. "That was Dr. Funk-n-Stine!"

"He said he would be back," added Bess.

Nancy hugged her puppy tight. She didn't want to believe in ghosts. But seeing was believing. And she was pretty sure she had just seen the ghost of Dr. Funk-n-Stine!

"Trick or treat, smell my feet!" Henderson sang as he ran through the school yard. "Give me something good to eat!"

Nancy watched as Henderson's red superhero cape flapped behind him. It was Halloween morning. Some of the kids at school were already dressed in their costumes.

"Okay, Clue Crew," George said. "What do we tell Shelby when we see her?"

"It's a no-brainer," Bess answered. "We tell her we saw a real live—I mean, real dead—ghost. Right, Nancy?"

"I guess." Nancy sighed. She'd been up all night trying to come up with a reason for seeing Dr. Funk-n-Stine. But she couldn't think of one.

"Well, I declare," Nadine's voice said. "I do believe it's the Clue Crew."

Nadine fluttered a lacy fan before her face

as she walked over. She was wearing an old-fashioned dress with puffy sleeves. The dress was so long it skimmed the ground.

"Pretty costume, Nadine," Nancy said. "Are you going trick-or-treating tonight?"

"I should say *not*!" Nadine replied. She tossed her long curls dramatically. "I am going to the Great Beyond—"

Nadine clapped the fan over her mouth. "I mean—I *am* going trick-or-treating!" she said. "And I can't wait!"

Nancy stared at Nadine as she ran off. Did she just say "the Great Beyond"?

"Bess, George," she said excitedly. She pulled the writing pad out of her backpack. "I think Nadine just gave us a new clue."

"What clue?" George asked.

"Nadine said she's going to a place called the Great Beyond," Nancy explained. "And we know she's not a ghost."

"Ghost? Did you say ghost?" asked a voice.

Nancy spun around and saw Shelby.

"Why didn't you tell me you saw a ghost?" Shelby asked. She then pointed to the pad in Nancy's hand. "What's that?"

"It's Nancy's Ghosts and No Ghosts columns," Bess explained. "So far the Ghosts column has the most clues."

"Not anymore," Nancy said. "I came up with a good reason for almost every Ghosts clue. Look at them, Shelby."

Shelby waved Nancy's list away. Then she began running through the school yard. "Listen up, everybody!" she yelled. "The Clue Crew proved that Dudley's studio really *is* haunted. So Dudley the Science Dude is innocent!"

"Great," Nancy muttered. "Now everyone at school will believe in ghosts."

"Does this mean the case is closed?" Bess asked.

"It is for Shelby," George said. "Now let's go on the monkey bars and figure out our trick-or-treat game plan."

The girls headed toward the monkey bars.

Nancy could see Shelby telling everyone about Dudley. She hadn't looked so happy in days!

George is right, Nancy thought. *The case is closed for Shelby. And I guess that's what counts.*

"Remember," Nancy said, "we're only allowed to go into houses we know."

"Check," George said.

It was four thirty in the afternoon. Nancy, Bess, and George were allowed to go trick-or-treating alone while it was still light outside.

The girls were wearing their costumes for the third time since Friday. Nancy and Bess wore sweaters under their costumes. George wore a sweatshirt under her tin cans.

"Our trick-or-treat bags are already half-full," Bess said happily. "And we just got started."

They turned onto Rowan Street and walked down the block.

"Neat!" Nancy said. "Look how many houses on this street are decorated for Halloween."

George pointed to an old gray house with

chipping paint and broken shutters. A jack-o'-lantern grinned at them from a porch.

"That one doesn't need decorations," she said. "It already looks haunted!"

Nancy gave a little groan. "No more ghost hunting, please. It's time to hunt for candy bars."

"And boxes of raisins!" Bess added with a hop.

"Yeah!" said George. "And sticky, gooey caramel apples—"

CREAK! The Clue Crew froze as the door of the old gray house opened slowly.

"Somebody lives in there?" Bess gasped.

"Who?" whispered George.

The girls slipped behind a giant oak tree on the sidewalk. They peeked out and watched a man step out of the house. He was wearing a dingy white lab coat and clunky black boots. His hair fuzzed out like a dandelion puff.

"It's Dr. Funk-n-Stine!" Bess hissed.

"He's not wearing his orange lab coat," George whispered. "And his hair looks whiter than in the pictures. How do we know it's him?"

The man locked his door. Then he turned and stepped off his warped wooden porch.

"There's only one way to find out," Nancy told the others. "We have to follow him."

CHAPTER EIGHT

Monsters in the House

Nancy huddled with Bess and George behind the tree. She could hear the man's feet crunching through leaves as he walked past them.

"What if he goes farther than our five-block rule?" Bess whispered.

"Then we're out of luck," replied Nancy.

The Clue Crew followed quietly. But when one of George's tin cans clanged against a fence, the man whirled around. Nancy, Bess, and George froze in their tracks.

"Um . . . trick-or-treat!" George blurted.

The man smiled. He reached into his pocket, pulled something out, and tossed it at the girls. George reached out her hand and caught it.

"Have a groovy Halloween, kids!" the man said. He gave a little wave and kept on walking.

"What is it?" Nancy asked George.

George opened her hand and gulped.

It was a pack of Baxter's Licorice Gum!

"He *is* Dr. Funk-n-Stine!" Bess gasped.

"Come on," Nancy said. "Let's not lose him."

George dropped the pack of gum in her bag. Then the girls trailed after Dr. Funk-n-Stine.

"He's heading toward River Street," Bess said. "Maybe he's going to haunt the TV station again."

Dr. Funk-n-Stine stopped suddenly. The girls stopped too. They watched quietly as he opened a gate and walked into a front yard.

Nancy, Bess, and George took a few steps

forward for a closer look. The yard was over-grown with weeds and dotted with tombstones. Nancy saw a sign post but couldn't make out the words because they were covered with vines. Behind the sign was a house that looked even creepier than Dr. Funk-n-Stine's. Its windows were dirty and broken. A notice on the door read ENTER IF YOU DARE!

The door of the house opened. A green-faced ghoul wearing a black cape and hood stepped out. He smiled at Dr. Funk-n-Stine as he walked up the path.

"Happy Halloween, Artie," said the ghoul.

"Thanks, Elliot," Dr. Funk-n-Stine said back. He gave the ghoul a little wave as he entered the house.

Nancy was puzzled. Whose house was this?

"Look!" Bess said. She pointed to their class-mate Kevin walking toward the house. Kevin was dressed as a pirate and held his mother's hand. "Kevin and his mom are going inside. What kind of a house could it be?"

The ghoul turned toward the sidewalk. He grinned at the girls with rotten teeth and said, "Come in. We've been *dying* to meet you!"

"Um, no thanks," Bess squeaked. "We've got enough candy for tonight."

The girls were about to run when they heard a scream.

A flurry of goose bumps raced up Nancy's arms and legs. She'd know that scream anywhere.

"Nadine Nardo! She's in that house and she's in trouble!"

"We have to help her," George said.

"What about our rules?" Bess asked. "We don't know anyone in that creepy house."

"We know Kevin and his mom," Nancy reminded her.

Another scream.

"We know Nadine, too," George said. "Let's go!"

The girls ran past the ghoul into the house.

"I knew you'd change your mind," the ghoul said. "Have a frightfully good time."

The girls followed the scream down a long dark hallway. As they swatted cobwebs aside, they didn't see Nadine or Kevin and his mom. But they did see skeletons and bats bouncing up and down from the ceiling, and portraits of people in old-fashioned clothes hanging on the wall.

Nancy glanced at a portrait of a man wearing a top hat. Suddenly the man reached up, tipped his hat, and said, "Happy Halloween!"

A grandfather clock gonged as they raced past it. A vampire popped out from behind the clock. He bared his fangs and growled, "Must be time for a snack!"

The hall led straight into a big room. The room was dark, but Nancy could see a suit of armor in the middle and a door in each of the walls.

"Nadine might be in one of those rooms," Nancy said, her heart racing.

The girls inched toward the nearest door. It creaked as Nancy pulled it open. As they

looked inside they gasped. Inside the velvet-draped room were monsters popping spiders and worms into their mouths!

"You're just in time for dinner!" one roared. "I hope you like meatballs and earthworms!"

Nancy slammed the door. "No Nadine in there," she said nervously. "Thank goodness."

The girls heard music behind the next door. George pulled it open and they peered inside. A werewolf smiled at them from behind a piano. His hairy fingers flew across the keys as he sang, "Bluuuue Moooon!"

George slammed the door shut. "This place is too weird," she said with a shudder. "Where is Nadine, anyway?"

"Maybe Dr. Funk-n-Stine has her!" Bess cried. "Maybe he's doing some weird experiments on her in a laboratory!"

"But where *is* Dr. Funk-n-Stine?" Nancy asked.

CREEEEAK! The girls spun around. The suit of armor's arm clanked as it pointed to one more door.

"Th-th-thanks!" Nancy stammered.

A white mist floated out from beneath the door. Bess pulled the door open. The mist swirled around their feet as they walked inside.

"Where are we?" asked Bess.

Nancy held her breath as she looked around. They were in another laboratory. This one had stone walls and all kinds of machines crackling with electricity. On a shelf stood glass jars filled with stuff that looked like brains. A raven sat perched inside a cage squawking, "Nevermore. Nevermore. Nevermore."

"What's that for?" Bess asked. She pointed to a long table in the middle of the room. Next to it was a lever.

"That reminds me of a movie I saw," said George.

"What movie?" Nancy asked.

"*Frankenstein*," George replied. "It was about a mad scientist who built a monster right in his lab!"

George hopped up on the table. She lay down flat.

"George!" Nancy said. "Don't touch anything—"

"The monster was dead at first," George said.

"But then Dr. Frankenstein pulled a lever. And the table rose all the way to the ceiling."

"You mean like this?" Bess asked. She grabbed the lever and pulled it all the way back.

The table and George began to rise.

"Not funny, Bess!" George called down. "You can stop this thing now."

The table rose higher and higher—too high for George to jump. Bess gripped the lever with all her might.

"I can't stop it!" Bess cried. "It's stuck!"

CHapTeR NiNe

Write Away

Nancy and Bess both grabbed the lever and pulled hard. But it was no use. The lever didn't budge!

"Get me down!" George shouted.

Suddenly another pair of hands grabbed the lever. Nancy spun around. It was Dr. Funk-n-Stine!

Nancy and Bess stepped aside as Dr. Funk-n-Stine pulled the lever back. The table began to drop slowly.

"Sorry," George said, hopping off the table.

"It's not your fault," Dr. Funk-n-Stine said. "If my

boss found out I left this room, I'd be toast!"

"Ghost?" Bess gasped.

"Not ghost—toast!" Dr. Funk-n-Stine said. He unwrapped a piece of licorice gum and popped it into his mouth.

"Then you're not a ghost?" George asked.

"Nope," Dr. Funk-n-Stine replied. "My career may be dead—but not me."

"But your website said you went to the Great Beyond," Nancy said.

"And I did!" Dr. Funk-n-Stine said with a smile. "Welcome to the Great Beyond Haunted Halloween House!" Then he leaned over and whispered, "And it's not really haunted."

Nancy smiled. Dr. Funk-n-Stine had just answered a very important question. But she still had more.

"Why did Dudley's studio look like your Groovy Mad Lab?" Nancy asked. "Are you having a Halloween party?"

Dr. Funk-n-Stine shook his head. "The station decided to have a Dr. Funk-n-Stine reunion show," he said. "I knew I'd be back someday."

"Is that why we heard your music?" asked George.

"Probably," Dr. Funk-n-Stine said. "I was trying out my old music tapes in the back."

Nancy, Bess, and George traded smiles.

"So that's why all those old clothes were in that room," Nancy said. "And why those test tubes fizzled over last Saturday."

"What test tubes?" Dr. Funk-n-Stine asked. "I wasn't at the TV station last Saturday."

Nancy stared at Dr. Funk-n-Stine. "You weren't?" she asked. "Then how . . . what . . . ?"

George grabbed Nancy's arm. "We'd better go," she said. "We have to be home before it gets dark, remember?"

Bess twirled on her toe. "Can you guess what we're all dressed up as, Dr. Funk-n-Stine?" she asked.

"Sure!" Dr. Funk-n-Stine said. "I see a ballerina, a dragon, and . . . a recycling machine!"

George sighed. "I'm a robot."

The girls thanked Dr. Funk-n-Stine for his help. Then they walked out of the lab and into the hall.

"So Dr. Funk-n-Stine isn't a ghost!" Bess declared.

The girls stopped short at the sound of a scream.

When Nancy whirled around, she saw Nadine running down the hall in her old-fashioned dress.

"Help!" Nadine shouted. "I've been bitten by a vampire!"

"Hi, Nadine," said Nancy.

Nadine stopped running. "Oh . . . hi," she said.

"What are you doing here?" George asked.

"I won a screaming contest at the mall last week," Nadine answered. "The prize was a chance to work at the Great Beyond."

"Why didn't you tell us?" Bess asked.

"I had to keep it a secret," Nadine said with a shrug. "Or no one would be scared when they saw me."

"We *were* scared, but not anymore," Nancy

said. "Dr. Funk-n-Stine told us all about the Great Beyond."

"It's not that great," Nadine whispered. "Truth . . . I'd rather be trick-or-treating."

Nancy, Bess, and George dodged dancing skeletons, falling cobwebs, and a zombie cheerleader as they made their way to the main door. They even ran into Kevin and his mom and some other classmates.

When they were finally outside, Bess sighed with relief. "Now we know Dr. Funk-n-Stine is not a ghost!" she said.

"But we still don't know why those beakers bubbled," Nancy said. "Or who wrote the formula that disappeared. Or who messed up Dudley's experiments last Friday."

"Maybe we'll never know," George said. She knelt down to tie her sneaker lace. Suddenly her eyes widened.

"What's wrong?" said Bess.

"Do you remember that Dudley and Kirby both signed my sneaker?" George asked.

"Sure," Nancy said.

George pointed to her right sneaker. "Dudley's autograph is still here," she said. "But Kirby's autograph . . . has disappeared!"

CHAPTER TEN

Monster Bash!

Nancy looked to see where George was pointing. Sure enough, Kirby's autograph was no longer where he'd written it.

"It disappeared just like the science formula disappeared," said George. "How did that happen?"

"Kirby must have used a pen with disappearing ink," Bess figured.

Nancy remembered when Kirby signed George's sneaker. He had used his own pen.

"You guys," Nancy said slowly, "do you think Kirby wrote his autograph *and* the science formula?"

"Why would Kirby write a science formula?"

Bess wondered. "It's not like he works on experiments."

"Maybe he does," George said. "Remember the day Kirby's face was covered with gray smudges? And his hair was sticking up like a porcupine's?"

"Yes, so?" Nancy asked.

"Static electricity makes hair stand up," George explained. "Maybe Kirby was doing his own experiments."

"But it's Dudley's show, not his," Bess pointed out.

"Kirby said he wants his own show someday," Nancy remembered. "He could have been practicing or something."

"No wonder his face was dirty." Bess giggled. "He must have been making a huge mess!"

Mess?

The girls stared at one another as it suddenly clicked. *"Dudley's messed-up science experiments!"* they chimed together.

Nancy wasn't sure if Kirby worked on Dudley's

experiments too. But she was determined to find out!

"Let's go back to the TV station after school tomorrow," Nancy suggested. "But this time we won't look for ghosts. We'll look for Kirby Kessler."

"I can't believe you put jellybeans in your tuna sandwich today, George," called Bess from her bike.

"What else am I going to do with all the candy I got last night?" George called back.

Nancy pedaled her bike behind her friends. It was Wednesday afternoon. As soon as school ended, the girls had run home for their bikes. Then they rode alongside Hannah on her bike to the TV station.

"I'll stay outside and watch your bikes," Hannah offered. "But don't be too long. You have homework to do."

The Clue Crew burst through the door of the TV station. When Beatrice the guard saw them, she groaned under her breath. "Now what?" she asked.

Nancy saw Dudley passing through the lobby. "Hi, Dudley," she called. "We were at your show last Friday."

"Oh, *that* show." Dudley groaned. "I still don't know why everything went wrong."

"We think we do," said Nancy. "That's why we'd like to see Kirby Kessler."

"I've been looking for Kirby myself," Dudley told the girls. "But I think I know how we can find him."

The girls followed Dudley through a door. Inside a dark room were computers, a switchboard, and a whole wall covered with TV monitors.

"This is the control room," Dudley explained. He smiled at a woman sitting behind the switchboard. "And this is Claudia, the assistant director. Claudia, turn on the studio monitors, please."

Claudia flipped some switches. A picture of a

different studio appeared on each of the monitors. Kirby was not inside any of them.

"One more," said Claudia. She flipped another switch. The set for a cooking show appeared on the last monitor.

"There's Kirby!" George said.

Kirby was standing behind a counter. He held up two bottles, looked straight into the camera, and said, "Yo! Give it up for me— Kirby the Science Kid!"

"He's doing his own show!" gasped Claudia.

Kirby poured a white powder into a bottle.

"Today we're making an awesome carbon dioxide gas!" he announced.

"He's pouring in too much," Dudley exclaimed. "It's going to blow!"

Dudley and the girls shot out of the control room and raced down the hall. But as they burst into the studio—

BOOM! FIZZZZZ! Everyone jumped as a small white cloud puffed out of the bottle.

"Pee-ew!" Nancy said, squeezing her nose.

"What a stink!" George declared.

"What are you doing, Kirby?" said Dudley. "You're not allowed to touch anything unless you're helping me."

"That's the problem." Kirby sighed. "I'm tired of being second banana. When I have my own show, I'm going to be the star!"

He brushed some powder off his sleeve. "I guess I just need a little more practice," he said.

"Did you ever practice on Dudley's experiments, Kirby?" Nancy demanded.

"Like last Friday?" George added.

"What are you, some kind of detectives?" asked Kirby.

"The best!" Bess said with a smile.

"Then you'd better tell them the truth, Kirby," Dudley said. "Go ahead."

Kirby heaved a big sigh. "Okay," he said. "I snuck into the studio before the show started so I could try out those experiments."

Kirby explained how he left the lid off the bat house after he fed them. And how he replaced the egg he cracked with a raw one. And how he refilled the bottles with too much vinegar and baking soda.

"They were accidents," Kirby said. "But not all my experiments are duds. I whipped up my own disappearing ink formula, and it really works!"

Kirby held up his pen.

"We know all about it," said Nancy.

The girls were about to present the note and the sneaker when Dudley grabbed the pen from Kirby's hand.

"Disappearing ink, huh?" Dudley said. "How

would you like to make some on my show next week, Kirby?"

"Wow! It's a deal," Kirby exclaimed.

"Wait a minute, Dudley," George said with a frown. "Our class couldn't be on your Halloween show, thanks to Kirby."

"Sorry," Kirby said.

"Can we come back for another show?" Bess asked.

Dudley scratched his chin thoughtfully. "I have a better idea," he said. "This guy named Dr. Funk-n-Stine needs an audience of kids for his show. Ever hear of him?"

"Does this answer your question?" Nancy asked. She turned to her friends and they began to sing: "Get up, get groooovy!"

"I guess that means yes!" Dudley laughed.

A few weeks later Mrs. Ramirez's third-grade class was back at

WRIV-TV. But this time they weren't wearing their Halloween costumes. They had on cool clothes from the 1970s!

The girls' platform shoes clunked as they danced to the beat of Dr. Funk-n-Stine's Groovy Mad Lab.

"I told you I didn't believe in ghosts!" Nancy shouted over the music. "Well . . . most of the time."

Shelby and Deirdre danced over. Both girls were wearing tie-dyed dresses with wide sleeves.

"Listen to this, you guys," Shelby said. She turned to Deirdre and said, "Go ahead. Spill."

"Okay, so Dudley *is* a real scientist," Deirdre admitted. "But Dr. Funk-n-Stine is totally cool."

"You mean *groovy*!" George said.

"Whatever," Deirdre sang as she danced away.

"Does this mean the Dudley the Science Dude Fan Club is a go?" Nancy asked Shelby.

Shelby shook her head. "I have a new favorite TV star," she answered. She nodded at Dr. Funk-n-Stine, who was pouring some ingredients into test tubes. "He may look a little creepy, but he's the real deal!"

A TV camera rolled past Henderson and Marcy as they pretended to dance like space aliens.

"I'm glad our class is finally on TV," Bess said. "And I'm glad the Clue Crew solved another case."

"You really are great detectives," Shelby said. "How do you do it?"

"I guess we have mysteries down to a science," Nancy replied with a smile.

George wiggled her fingers and laughed. "You mean *mad* science!" she said.

IT'S A STRING THING!

(String of Ghosts or Jack-O'-Lanterns)

It's no mystery that Halloween is more fun with cool decorations—like a string of ghosts or smiling pumpkins to hang across your room or window. Not only are they fun to make, they're as easy as pie . . . pumpkin pie!

You Will Need:

Construction paper (orange and black for pumpkins, white and black for ghosts)

Crayons or markers

Scissors

Glue, tape, or staples

A long piece of green or black yarn or string

On Your Mark . . .
Get Set . . . Ghost!

❀ Draw a ghost on white paper, or a pumpkin on orange paper. Don't forget to draw a long stem on the top. The stems will be folded over later when it's time to hang up your ghosts or pumpkins.

❀ Cut out your ghost or pumpkin. Use black paper to make eyes, a nose, and a mouth. Or use your crayons or markers to draw them on.

✷ Fold the ghost's stem all the way back. Fold the pumpkin's stem halfway back. Now hook the ghost or pumpkin onto a long string or yarn (black yarn for ghost, green yarn for pumpkin).

✷ Tape, glue, or staple the back of the stem to hold it in place.

✷ Add more ghosts and pumpkins in all shapes and sizes—until you're ready to string up your creepy creation!

More Ideas: Mix up ghosts and pumpkins on the same string. Or go wild with black cats or bats. When it comes to Halloween, THE MORE THE SCARIER!

Scott County Public Library
Georgetown, Kentucky 40324